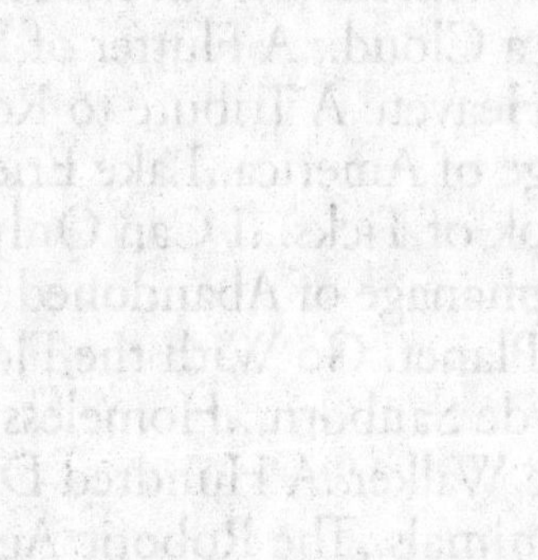

good deed rain

51 Books by Allen Frost

...Ohio Trio...Bowl of Water...Another Life...
...Home Recordings...The Mermaid Translation...
...The Selected Correspondence of Kenneth
Patchen...The Wonderful Stupid Man...
...Saint Lemonade...Playground...Roosevelt...
...5 Novels...The Sylvan Moore Show...
...Town in a Cloud...A Flutter of Birds Passing
Through Heaven: A Tribute to Robert Sund...
..At the Edge of America..Lake Erie Submarine..
...The Book of Ticks...I Can Only Imagine...
...The Orphanage of Abandoned Teenagers...
..Different Planet..Go With the Flow: A Tribute
to Clyde Sanborn...Homeless Sutra...
..The Lake Walker..A Hundred Dreams Ago..
..Almost Animals..The Robotic Age..Kennedy..
...Fable...Elbows & Knees: Essays and Plays...
...The Last Paper Stars...Walt Amherst is Awake...
....When You Smile You Let in Light....
...Pinocchio in America...Florida...
..Blue Anthem Wailing..The Welfare Office..
...Island Air...Imaginary Someone...
....Violet of the Silent Movies....
...The Tin Can Telephone...Heaven Crayon...
..Old Salt..A Field of Cabbages..River Road..
...The Puttering Marvel...Something Bright...
...The Trillium Witch...Cosmonaut...
...Thriftstore Madonna...Half a Giraffe...

..Lexington Brown & The Pond Projector..

LEXINGTON BROWN
& THE POND PROJECTOR

by ALLEN FROST

Illustrated by AARON GUNDERSON

Writing: Allen Frost
Cover & Illustrations: Aaron Gunderson
Page 104 from *A Hundred Dreams Ago* (2017)
Page 114-115 from *The Book of Ticks* (2018)
Cover Production: Fred Sodt
Quote: Stephen King, *IT*, Viking Penguin Inc., New York, 1986
Apple: TFK!

For Donald J. Sobol & Leonard Shortall

LEXINGTON BROWN
&
THE POND PROJECTOR

Allen Frost

Good Deed Rain ◊ Bellingham, Washington ◊ 2022

Banks erected inside their heads where once magic picture-palaces had stood.

—Stephen King

CONTENTS

Lexington Brown, Dream Inventor — 15

Lexington Brown Takes on the Town — 22

Lexington Brown Gathers the Gang — 30

Lexington Brown Reads the Signs — 37

Lexington Brown Travels in Time — 42

Lexington Brown & The Sleeping Kid — 47

Lexington Brown Sets the Stage — 54

Lexington Brown Goes to City Hall — 61

Lexington Brown Makes a Scene — 68

Lexington Brown at the Aquarium — 79

Solutions — 85

INTRODUCTION

It's hard to say exactly how this book started, although I can make a good guess. It was June. At the time I was rereading Part 2 of *IT*, when I found my old copy of *Encyclopedia Brown Strikes Again* in a box in my parents' basement. That was the inspiration I needed for writing what happened here. Let me also thank Mantan Moreland for creating Birmingham Brown. Feel free to think of this as a black and white movie made by Republic Pictures in 1941...*Lexington Brown and The Pond Projector*...

—AF, Bellingham, June 27, 2021

INVENTIONS BY
BROWN
13 CLOVER AVENUE
LEXINGTON BROWN, INVENTOR
IDEAS EVERY DAY

LEXINGTON BROWN, DREAM INVENTOR

The Brown's house is in a green yard, with apple trees and its very own pond. That pool of water, as you will see, becomes the starting point of this latest Lexington Brown adventure, but not quite yet. Just wait.

It had once been a family house, his mother, his father and him, but now he was the only one left and the property was his and he was the lonely king of it all.

So far it was a calm, sunny first day of June and the blue air was furred with drifting cottonwood seeds, soft as snow. They stuck to the roof and eaves of the house and lay snug in the leaves. The gravel driveway was littered with white catkins here and there. They pawed like rabbits all the way past the garage, to the backyard pond.

Every morning Lexington Brown was drawn

to that spot. He was sort of haunted by it. First, he would see it in the kitchen window while he prepared his coffee, then he would oftentimes go outside and sit beside it for a while. Especially if the weather was nice like it was today.

Forty years ago, he and his two friends dug that hole in the ground, filled it with water, bucket by bucket and garden hose, and he named it Avalon Pond. He had big plans. He always did. Back then, ideas came to him like bright flocks of songbirds.

He walked through the grass in his moccasins. The dew slapped on like paint.

The pond waited for him. It had continued to grow, gradually, filled by years of rain.

The little dock he made a long time ago needed repairs. Only one plank reached to the end anymore and it dipped halfway with a green puddle holding it down in the middle. It knew he would never dare to cross it. He would have to be a carefree ten-year-old again, hopping in sneakers.

A redwing blackbird chimed from the cattails.

An old dining room chair sat beside the shore. Over the years the chairs would come and go, he lost count of them, they lasted until the weather got to them. Once they broke or warped too badly, he would start stopping at garage sales or Goodwill. This one was good, solid, straight-backed, with sturdy legs that pinned it to the muddy bank.

He often thought about his last invention as he watched the water. He couldn't help it—he still thought it was a good idea, even if it lay under ten feet of water.

An inventor is someone who has an idea to change the world. With Lexington Brown, that was easy, he had ideas all the time.

Lexington Brown wasn't sitting there for more than a few minutes before he noticed something strange. Light smudged in the depths. It wavered the way moonlight shimmers through a dark canopy, and right away he knew what it was. Afterall, he put it there.

Left to the murky water.

But what miracle had brought it back to life?

That he didn't know. A tremor? An electric pulse, some magnetic disturbance? Maybe it was a frog who knew how to work the controls, the dials and reels…a frog who knew how to focus a beam of light just right, so it formed pictures on the algae covered screen.

Lexington Brown was on his feet. He had to take a look, but he wasn't about to try his luck on that old plank of a pier. He had a better way to get out there.

He had a rowboat. It was crowded by horsetails waiting for the boat to move so they could shake like a hundred Shetland ponies. Lexington flipped it over. The boat had been on that spot for so long, underneath was a dirt shadow of itself. The oars clacked, stowed away under the bench seat, rattling as he dragged the boat. He could have been an old pirate returning to sea.

He sunk footsteps into the sod becoming mud at the edge of the wetlands. Hobbled by the plexiglass weight he was pulling into the rushes and reeds, cracking stalks aside. Carp flapped and thrashed showing their yellow scales. A heron beat to wing.

The blackbird on the other side of the pond flew off as Lexington tipped the boat. It hit like breaking glass and made a ring of waves. He steadied it and wobbled into it, onto the seat. The last time he rowed was when he exiled his creation to the bottom of the world.

When Lexington was ten years old, it was a dream of his to show movies underwater. He was sure it would catch on. People laughing, splashing, diving down. He pictured theater seats with helmets the audience could wear, hoses that would snake up into

the air. Off the coast, there could be drive-ins with submarines parked on the sand. Imagine watching a screen with herring swimming around you. Ponds were everywhere in town, all you had to do was dig to find one. He envisioned taking movies to all of them, there could be a vaudeville circuit underwater. He felt sure The Pond Projector could have made history, the same way the eggbeater did.

Lexington stopped rowing and looked over the edge. He held the oars up so they dripped little diamonds off. At first, a blue sky was reflected on the surface, then it was happening, he was vanishing. He was looking through the sky into the pond world. The swamp clung to him and pulled his attention deeper, gone, under the lily pads waving over in the wind.

Below the surface a few fathoms down is what he's looking for, plain as a mirage, bent and lit by green beams of sun. A shoal of fish meandered past. Their formation flew above the cement projection booth and the rays of the movie it was showing. It was just the way he dreamed it was meant to be. All it needed was an audience.

The glow disappeared. That was it for the movie. As if chairs in rows were rocking back, bubbles shot to the surface and burst around the rowboat. Round little green leaves small as penny rivets swerved and spread again to cover the disturbance and the dissolving silhouettes below.

A moth floated on the pond. He dipped an oar under it and lifted it and like a cook with a spatula, tapped it safely into the prow. Lexington Brown was back in the world above water. The painted view was chopped by digging paddles as he turned the boat around. Why was the projector alerting him? There had to be a reason. Somehow, he decided he had to retrieve his invention. It wouldn't be easy, but he knew he would think of a way.

HOW DID LEXINGTON BROWN
RECOVER THE POND PROJECTOR?

*(Turn to page 85 for the solution to
"Lexington Brown, Dream Inventor")*

LEXINGTON BROWN
TAKES ON THE TOWN

When he was ten, Lexington Brown was a dynamo, bright and cheerful, as sure of himself as a spring flower. He had the sort of glow that made you happy to have him around and listening to him was like music on the radio. That summer long ago, he sat in the kitchen with a typewriter on top of that red Formica table and wrote a letter. He read it aloud for his parents to hear:

```
Dear City Council,
My name is Lexington Brown.
I am ten years old. I am in the fifth grade.
I want to be an inventor when I grow up.
Until then, I want to learn as much as I
can.
So I'm making inventions all the time.
My latest invention is The Pond Projector.
```

I think everyone will want to experience
this.
Let me explain:
We have ponds all around our town. Every
neighborhood has one. Most of the time we
just walk around them. But what if we made
them a movie experience!
What if we showed movies underwater?
Wouldn't people think that was neat?
I have a great invention that makes that
happen.
Please stop by my house at 13 Clover Avenue
for a demonstration.

Sincerely,
Lexington Brown

After he sealed it in an envelope, that very evening
he took his letter to the blue mailbox on the corner
and dropped it in. He heard the small whispery sound
of its dark landing. Then he shut the metal drawer.
It would take a couple days before he got a reply. In
the meantime, he typed another letter to one of his
heroes, one of the world's great inventors, Francis
Thomas Drysdale.

23

Dear Mr. Drysdale,
I have been wanting to write you for a
long time. I am a ten year old inventor.
I hope we meet one day when I'm older but
this letter will get there faster.
You are my favorite inventor. I have
checked out your book fifteen times from
the library. I keep looking for 'Water
and Other Frequencies' in bookstores but
it must be out of print.
I don't make money with my inventions yet
but I have saved some from chores.
Do you know where I can find your book?

                    Sincerely
                    Lexington Brown

A week went by. He watched that mailbox, he
was practically wired to it. He listened for the purr
of the white truck slowing down into the shoulder.
Wherever Lexington was, in the house or the garage,
or out in the yard, he would come running. After

another day, on a raining evening after 6:30, he ran past his mom and slammed the door on the way out. The mail truck was still there as he ran across the lawn. It slowly picked up speed and the driver waved.

Lexington's sneakers slapped across the sidewalk to the silver mailbox. He figured the letter inside would change his life. Smart as he was, what does a ten-year-old know?

The envelope was from the Coordinator of City Affairs. Drops of rain dotted the page as Lexington read it on his way back to the house. He bumped the door open and cried, "They want to see it!" and in two days that seemed to take forever, the pond in the backyard had visitors—the city coordinator and a secretary, the owner of the Avalon Theatre downtown, a reporter from the *Herald*, and for support, Lexington's best friends Ida and Curly.

Lexington rowed his first visitor. He let the rowboat float while he examined the water. Sometimes it was the sky reflected on the surface, blue and a few clouds, but Lexington could also switch channels and he would be looking through the mirror and he could see the weedy bottom of Avalon Pond. He rested his elbows on the edge of the boat and watched the way the weeds went slowly back and forth in the current.

A fish sparkled like a dime. Another one joined it. Twenty cents. Then he saw the projection booth, a submerged hollow block of concrete sealed with a movie projector inside.

He dug an oar into water to hover above it.

On the bench seat next to him was a TV remote control. When he pointed it at the water and pressed a button, the film started to roll.

One at a time he took each visitor out onto the pond to look down, starting with the owner of the Avalon Theatre. That was only fitting, Lexington said, as the pond was named in honor of that palace on Champion Street.

While he rowed back to shore, Lexington Brown's invention rewound the reel and was ready to play again. Everything went so well, he thought.

But tomorrow's *Herald* told the story another way, in a little story on page 8.

"LOCAL BOY GOES LOCO. Ten-year-old Lexington Brown of Clover Avenue has invented the craziest contraption this reporter has ever seen." It went on. There was more. It ended with, "Unless you're a mermaid, you won't have any use for The Pond Projector."

The City Councilor called him that night and

explained, "You want people to get in pondwater to watch a movie? That doesn't sound like an appealing entertainment, young Mr. Brown."

They didn't want his invention and that hurt. Lexington left it shipwrecked in the pond. "What's the point of recovering it?" he thought and left it alone like the Titanic.

Lexington Brown wouldn't let it get him down. He already read Drysdale's biography three times and he knew every great inventor had to put up with this. It was part of the job. So he snipped that newspaper article and nailed it on the cedar Rejections board in the garage. That board was filling up. Most of his inventions were pinned like dried butterflies. There was an exception though—above his desk, he had a framed patent for The Birdsong Thermometer. That was his success story. He kept the prototype on his windowsill. It was just like a regular thermometer, but the red level told him how many birds were singing. Lexington thought it was great, he liked the thrill it gave him. And The Brooklyn Office of Patents & Trademarks agreed.

That was a hard day, but he had his friends.

Ida appeared at the open garage door, "Hey Lex.," and walked in carrying a big wrapped present. "I thought you could use some cheering up."

He grinned. "Well, well, look at that."

She really surprised him, especially when he took off the taped paper. It was a pair of black rubber swimming flippers, painted with red, pink and white hearts.

She laughed at the look on his face. "What do you think?"

He really didn't know.

"For swimming in the pond," she said. "Or wherever."

He never got another present like that.

Curly showed up later too. He was on his bike. He was in the neighborhood, he said. He was his usual self, joking and doing his best to catch Lexington laughing.

They were his best friends. He could always count on them.

When he went back to the house, his mother called him over. She held an envelope. She was smiling.

Lexington couldn't believe it. His own name typed on the envelope by Francis Thomas Drysdale! With all The Pond Projector drama, he forgot that he wrote to his hero. He hoped Drysdale would have something good to say. Maybe a signed copy of *Water and Other*

Frequencies was on the way. What excitement! Part of him was almost afraid to open the letter.

WHAT DID THE FAMOUS INVENTOR TELL HIM?

(Turn to page 87 for the solution to "Lexington Brown Takes on the Town")

LEXINGTON BROWN GATHERS THE GANG

Were someone as rational as Lexington Brown to believe in fate, he would have wondered about unseen hands steering him. First came the discovery of the long-gone drowned ghost of The Pond Projector. Next came a letter to him in the mail. It was stuffed in the box with a handful of slick coupons and ads.

Salutations Mr. Brown,

We read about your inventions in the Herald.

"The Pond Projector" sounds fascinating to us!

Not sure if you are aware, but the aquarium

is celebrating fifty years of serving fish to

the community. We would really like to have

a memorable event and we wonder if you would

Lexington laughed. "I always knew they'd find me." He read the letter again. "Look at that!…I knew it!" He chuckled and carried the mail up the driveway, around the side of the house. He dropped the other junk mail in an oil drum. Looking at the envelope again, he shook his head. It was great to see that smile, famously remembered by his family and his friends, Ida and Curly.

The sign on the garage door was faded but still readable.

INVENTIONS BY BROWN
13 Clover Avenue
Lexington Brown, Inventor
Ideas Every Day

You couldn't just open the door and walk in. A typewriter keyboard was attached to the door. It controlled the security bar on the other side. If you didn't type SWORDFISH, the door would stay locked.

He was still a little stung by that old *Herald* article. The reporter never understood The Pond Projector. Readers would have expected Lexington Brown to curl up and dry like a bee on a windowsill. The years would have turned the floor into an inch of dust and cobwebs after gloom took over that boy's invention factory. Luckily that wasn't true. Lexington Brown flicked the light switch and the place resembled the mind of Albert Einstein.

Lexington's projector was one of hundreds of inventions. He left a blanket covering it. What an unbelievable story this was! He wanted to write it down, as if it was another movie he and Ida and Curly could make. What an immortal struggle to resurrect it. First, he had to catch it. Floating above it, Lexington fished for the eye-hook on top of the cabinet. The line pulled along until it snagged. Lexington used the technology of the Egyptian pharaohs to get it to the garage. This time he expected the *Herald* to get it right, with the headline: THE POND PROJECTOR RETURNS!

The concrete looked good for being stuck underwater all that time. No cracks or apparent leaks. Algae had turned it green. Fortunately, the lens was still clear. In the desk drawer he still had the plans. He could build more Pond Projectors if they wanted him to. Every pond in town deserves The Pond Projector!

He loosened a side panel and carefully removed the cover.

The projector was prepared with the reel.

"How long has it been playing this same movie?" Lexington wondered. Or was it just that one morning, to get his attention? He was baffled. He didn't see any loose wires or wears. Whatever happened was part of a mysterious plan.

He went to his desk to write a letter to the aquarium.

When he sat down, it creaked like the skeleton of a chair. The desk was from his grandparents' house. It was an old office rolltop. He got a tack from one of the compartments and pinned the letter on the wall next to his framed patent.

"Will you look at that?" He studied the letter.

Then he thought, "Why write them and wait to hear back when I can make a telephone call?" The aquarium's number was embossed in the paper.

Another treasure in that rolltop desk was his

grandparent's 1940s telephone. It was made of black Bakelite. The receiver had weight to it, the dial turned stiffly, and he could hear the numbers rattle in his ear. Then another click as someone answered.

"Good afternoon, this is Gillian."

"Hi…Gillian. I'm Lexington Brown, I got your letter."

"Yes! Oh, I'm so happy to hear from you. What do you think about our idea? Do you still have your Pond Projector? Does is still work?"

He laughed. "Yes, yes. It's good as new!"

They had such a pleasant conversation, when he hung up Lexington Brown felt like Francis Thomas Drysdale. Better than that.

The chair groaned as he leaned over to open one of the drawers. He got a paper and a sharpened pencil. He reached for the telephone again. He really liked the feel of it. It made him think of the beautiful invented things.

The rotary dial had ten holes, the one after 9 was for the operator. Or at least it used to be. He wasn't sure who would answer these days, did they still have operators? They were a whooping crane on a desolate landscape. If the telephone book didn't make them extinct, computers make it easy to look anything up.

Who needed an operator anymore?

Lexington Brown did. His finger dialed the zero after nine.

WHY DID LEXINGTON BROWN CALL THE OPERATOR?

(Turn to page 88 for the solution to "Lexington Brown Gathers the Gang")

LEXINGTON BROWN
READS THE SIGNS

Owen Feathers was one of those unusual characters in town, not that Lexington Brown didn't consider himself part of their ranks. Except Owen had no house to sleep in, or garage, or for that matter a pond. Now that it was summer, he slept in the woods, only appearing a couple times a day. You might see him swaying like Dylan Thomas up the street.

"What happened to the sign that was here?" he asked Lexington. He described it with his hands in the air.

It looked like he shaped a billboard, or a poster glued to a fence that long ago turned into this rubbled over blackberry lot. "The sign," he repeated. There was also the possibility that it was nothing but a For Sale sign. Owen had a head full of bees, the buzz you hear when you dive underwater in a lake full of outboard motors. Owen's hands polished the air.

Then it hit him, and Lexington Brown was rushed back to 1974. Thanks to Owen Feathers' power of projection, Lexington saw the sign as plain as if it was there again. A big announcement was painted on a wooden board and planted like a door at the edge of the field. A circus show! Lexington was there again. It was night, spotlights crisscrossed the sky and he remembered kids from his school were there, including Owen Feathers. That's when Owen saw the tightrope walker up against the black sky. That's why the next day on the playground, Owen tried to stand at the top of the swing-set. After he fell off of it, he never stopped falling.

"The circus?" Lexington asked him.

Owen nodded. He looked up at where the acrobat was, but the sun was too bright, he covered his eyes.

"Alright," Lexington nodded. "Thanks for reminding me." Owen didn't answer, he might have fallen into that memory. Lexington let him stand in that shadow and left. A bird was singing. A nearby car was becoming scrap, the hood and doors open, a yawning metalwork relic. Believe it or not, the field was still there. The circus must have left it with magical powers to avoid the detection of real estate agents and banks. That thought had crossed Lexington's mind before. What if he could invent a ray, a beam from the invisible spectrum? He could point it at a field like this and all that could be seen would be a row of gray apartments. The treasures in the city could be saved that way. Why were these places always in danger of slipping away? Who was running things anyway? All his life Lexington Brown had been inventing a different world.

The path turned into matted grass and dried puddles. In the open air above him the swallows were diving and steering madly. Lexington started to whistle. The weeds at the edge of the path were crushed down. It was a distracted circle where a rabbit had been killed, some gray and white fur. The tall grass stalks leaned in closer as he walked.

For a while, it was like cutting through an ocean the way the wind furled over each rise and fall of the weeds. A songbird called from an apple tree, in the hard green bulbs on its branches. Then everything splashed onto worn ground that soon became cement.

Like a paperboy, Lexington Brown had his route.

He liked the path under trees, down alleys, backyards, sometimes barking dogs, sometimes cats that would come over to say hello, windchimes on porch corners, someone working on a car. He picked up a scrap of newsprint and read the words. He believed in messages and signs.

He and Ida and Curly found an undiscovered America in vacant lots. They took exploring expeditions to them. Ida wrote about each one in a notebook. Lexington wondered if she still had that. In his mind he could still see the pictures she drew. On one of those journeys Lexington invented The Human Bubble. A balloon that you wore, and you could float off the ground. Imagine the slow motion feeling of that. He asked Ida to draw that for him and he still remembered that page in her notebook. There he was in the bubble and a bird was sitting on top of it, riding along.

He wasn't surprised to realize Owen Feathers was drawn to these same places too. They both knew magic when they saw it. And Lexington was used to marvels along the way—that's how he looked at the world—nothing was ordinary, anything could happen and there's always room for something new.

Like what he saw next, on the gravel driveway. A crow held a snake in its beak and claw. It flapped and shook the snake around its head. It was an omen, it had to be. It took Lexington a moment then he forced a step. He liked garter snakes—he liked crows too, but he couldn't just watch this happen. Before he could tell his feet to pick up speed, the crow took off, carrying the snake. Lexington could only watch it go, twenty feet above a backyard fence. As he thought about what he saw, he recalled the same scene was also on the flag of Mexico. He tried to remember what that meant. It was a good thing, wasn't it? An Aztec legend, or the epic battle of good over evil. He reminded himself to look that up at the library.

Lexington Brown liked to let his mind wander while he walked. That's how people got ideas. You had to be aware, they could be anywhere. While he was drifting, Lexington's town was full of never-ending sights to see, and he could catch thoughts along the way.

He could relate to the rabbits, the clouds, the litter people left behind. Owen Feathers wasn't the only one seeing signs.

WHAT WILL HAPPEN TO OWEN FEATHERS?

(Turn to page 90 for the solution to "Lexington Brown Reads the Signs")

LEXINGTON BROWN
TRAVELS IN TIME

Lexington Brown watched the sky. He could have put his own strange flying machines up there. Instead of cranky propellor planes, or loud jets with sharp wings, there could have been saucers, floating bells, and things resembling dragonflies.

The airport was a half hour drive from Clover Avenue. He was anxious and nervous as he stood by the big window and waited for a dot to appear in the air. Forty years was a long time not to see someone. The plane would land, the people would walk out, and no matter what time had done, he knew he would know it was her.

He hoped she would recognize him. Just in case, he wore a red flower in his black jacket lapel. Didn't people do that in movies? A little speck moved out of the clouds. He couldn't believe she was coming all this way to see his invention again. She never forgot it either, he supposed.

The airplane gained form in the glass, turned to silver, moved like a bird gliding onto the far end of the runway. "Oh my…" Lexington breathed. Here he was, wearing a flower, waiting for a girl who was no longer a girl. He hadn't seen her since she flew away from this same airport when he was a boy. At the end of the fifth grade, her family moved away. Then they lost touch. Was it crazy to think they would have anything in common after all their experiences apart? She was on the plane. "Oh my…" he repeated. This was happening.

Speakers in the ceiling made it clear she was here. Lexington looked around quickly and saw he wasn't the only one waiting. Ever since they cleared the land, laid down the tarmac, raised the radar tower and put in these windows, people felt like him. A man with orange wands waved the plane in. The hum of the propellers shook the glass. They chopped and stopped. Lexington took a step backwards, looked at the door, took another step forward. He fidgeted with the flower and a red petal stuck to him.

By now the passengers were standing from their seats, getting their bags and books. Ida would be looking out her window, wondering what seeing

Lexington Brown again would be like. While she pulled her jacket tight, the red carnation in it shook. She told him she would be wearing that flower. He said he would be too.

Lexington had moved to the door and leaned his back against the wall. He was writing an idea in the pocket notebook he carried. There was a drawer full of those notebooks back home. When he looked out the window again, people were already stepping onto the ground. He didn't see Ida though. A lady carried a suitcase and birdcage. That was strange, Lexington thought, a bird flying in an airplane…And then, oh boy, his fingers tapped…There she was.

Of course she had the same white hair as him and favored wearing a sweater, same as him, but that was Ida and he felt such a relief to see her. She saw him in the waiting room and she waved and smiled and he did too. Ida used to light up near him, her smile and that laugh, and he didn't even know then how that was one of the best inventions ever. They were both laughing as she came in through the door. They couldn't help it, they felt like they each sailed different directions around the world and had just met where they started.

"Lex? Is that you?"

"How'd you know?"

"Oh Lex…I remember you."

The airport was only a floor leading to the door and the parking lot.

"Is that your truck?" Ida asked. She pointed at a Chevrolet that had been through the Cuban Missile Crisis.

He nodded, "That's my grandfather's truck." He pointed at the lettering on the door and read, "Jim McBrady. Construction."

"Jim McBrady," she said. Her voice was exactly the way he remembered.

"Let me get the door for you. It has to be charmed."

"Okay." She only had one bag. She could fit it next to her in the cab. If it wasn't already filled with cardboard wings, or boxes of springs.

Lexington lifted the door a little as he opened it, that was the secret. "Do you know," he said, "I miss those times when I used to go to your house. I liked your room." She would play records and he would tell her ideas for inventions. "Do you still have that Beatles poster? I can picture it on the wall."

She laughed, "Oh Lex, that was a million years ago! Who knows what happened to that?" She was pleased with old Jim McBrady. The seat was mended in a couple places with silver tape. On the dashboard were a couple sand dollars and some dry branches off a cedar tree. "Did you add an invention to Jim McBrady? It seems to be hiding something. Can it fly?"

"Fly? No, not that I know of. But you're right, I did, uhhh, customize the engine." He shut her door and patted the rusted side. She was in for a surprise. He bet she never drove in a truck powered by a 1979 basketball team.

"So you're still making your inventions?" she said as he joined her on the worn bench seat.

"Oh yes! Yes indeed." He held the key and said, "Just listen…"

WHAT DID IDA HEAR?

(Turn to page 92 for the solution to "Lexington Brown Travels in Time")

LEXINGTON BROWN
& THE SLEEPING KID

"Where are we?" Ida asked. "What are we doing in White Pond?" They were still twenty minutes from his house, in a whole other town.

"You'll see." He reached out the window and pressed a button on a post.

A woman answered the intercom, "Fine's Self Storage. If it's not fine, it won't do. How can I help with your self storage needs?"

Lexington said, "We're here to see Curly Bane."

The intercom rattled like broken shells and then buzzed as the gate unlocked.

Ida's eyes widened, "Curly? What's he doing here?"

Lexington shrugged. "This is the address the operator gave me."

Jim McBrady cheered itself along the curved driveway and parked before the brick three-story building. The Sonics were somewhere in the first quarter as the motor died.

Another woman met them at the steps. She wore a long white lab coat and a stethoscope necklace. "Welcome to Fine's Self Storage," she greeted them. "Won't you follow me? We have three plans for your consideration."

"Plans?"

"Technically there are four, but we don't recommend the fourth. It's the cheapest option and let's face it, you get what you pay for."

"Cheapest, eh?" He glanced at Ida. "That sounds like Curly alright."

"Curly Bane?" the woman soured. "Is that why you're here?"

"Where is he?" Ida said.

"The basement level. He's the only one there, he's the only one to opt for Plan D. You can't miss him."

"We can go right down?" Lexington asked her.

"Sure, be my guest. Maybe you can convince him to leave."

A stairway led up to two more floors, a door led down to the cellar.

"Okay then," Lexington said. He glanced at Ida as he opened the door. "Ladies first."

They descended wooden creaking stairs. It smelled

like Halloween. Ahead of them their footsteps echoed in the greenish wax museum pallor. The basement didn't need much light. There wasn't much there—a boiler, a bare floor, a stack of packing boxes and some spare furniture…and a bed with a boy in it.

Ida gasped and put her hands to her mouth. "Is that Curly?"

Lexington held her arm. "I think so…"

They stood beside the bed and Ida's breath hitched.

"Is he asleep?" Lexington whispered. "You think it's okay to wake him?"

Ida whispered, "This is the first time we've seen him in forty years and look at him! He's still a boy. What happened?"

"I don't know."

A wire ran from Curly's arm. It snaked across to the bedside table where it entered a switchbox. There were two settings on it: OFF and ON. "Look at that," said Lexington.

Ida shared an unspoken decision with Lexington, then she reached slowly across the table, past the waterglass and an old paperback entitled *Gallows Humor*, and she flicked the OFF button.

"Oh boy…" Lexington clasped his hands. "Here we go."

Curly—it really was him—stirred. Fine gears seemed to move through his arm as it bent. With his eyes still closed he muttered, "I don't want to go to school, ma."

Ida laughed, but she had to bite her lip. It was like seeing her own son in the hospital. "Curly, it's us! Lex and Ida."

He opened his eyes and blinked a few times. Gone were the days when he slept for years at a time, now he had to get up every month. He had to make rent. He had to leave the basement and go out looking for chores: fences that needed painting, windows washed, or lawns to be mown. If it was a Saturday, he would take his ukulele to the market and play for pennies.

"What happened to you guys?" he croaked.

"What happened to *you*, Curly? You never got older."

"I know. It's sort of a long story."

"Well, spill it!" Lexington said.

"Okay, but can you pass me that water first?" After he took a sip and handed it back, he began, "There was an accident when I was eleven. They put me to sleep with this machine. It kept me frozen this way until the future doctors would know how to save my life. A little more water?" He took the glass again. "I'm okay now. You can't see what happened to me, the doctors did a great job. So, I'm still eleven but it's forty years later." He yawned and rubbed his eyes. "Jeeze, it's something to see you guys…What are you doing here?"

Lexington explained how the projection booth had emerged from the depths of Avalon Pond. He told the kid about the letter from the aquarium and how they wanted him to bring his invention there and it sounded like he was telling a bedtime story about a scullery maid who goes to the castle in a pumpkin carriage.

"I always had faith in you!" Curly grinned.

"So can you come with us tomorrow to the aquarium?"

"I don't know…"

"What?" Ida chided. "Why not? Do you have a busy schedule?" Ida didn't see a calendar. Why would there be one?

"No," Curly replied, "I just like sleeping."

"Oh, Curly, don't be lazy! I flew a thousand miles to be here for Lex."

"Tomorrow, huh?" he sighed. He confessed that he was okay to leave Fine's Self Storage anytime, he just didn't want to. He explained that he liked dreams more than real life. He wanted to be asleep. He paid them to keep him that way. But when his two old friends said they would send him a cab, he grudgingly promised he would take it to the aquarium. The effort it took Curly to get through all the talking made him tired though. He struggled to keep his eyes open. "Can you hit the ON button for me?" he begged.

They said goodnight. Ida lay a hand on his forehead.

Curly could be their grandchild if you didn't know.

They left the boy in that waxy green basement and hurried outside.

Jim McBrady started with a ref's whistle and the crowd roared like surf. Anyone who lived in Seattle back then would have been cheering. There was enough excitement to push the truck fifty miles per hour.

Ida read the road sign aloud, "You are now leaving White Pond. Come back soon." She shook her head, "I don't think so." White Pond was a cold winter town. For a few months in the spring and summer though, it was green as a jungle and hot enough to melt the road and make heatwaves rise off the tar.

Jim McBrady continued, "Williams comes around, right to the floor. It's a four-point Sonic lead on that field goal by Gus Williams!"

WHAT WAS THE FINAL SCORE OF THE BASKETBALL GAME?

(Turn to page 93 for the solution to "Lexington Brown & The Sleeping Kid")

LEXINGTON BROWN
SETS THE STAGE

13 Clover Avenue was a welcome sight. Ida used to ride her bike here all the time, follow the driveway to the garage with the sign on the door and in she would go. She said, "Oh, it's just like I remember!" Daisies and buttercups popped around in the grass. Jim McBrady parked beside the red painted wall where Lexington's inventions were stored. "Can we go in there?"

"Sure."

Ida was out of the truck before him. "Look!" She ran her fingers over the keyboard. "Can I enter the code?"

"You remember it?"

"Of course I do!"

"Be my guest." After he made Ida his business partner, he gave her that secret password. In fifth grade, he expected he would need her math skills to keep track of the contracts and transactions and international exchanges.

The security bar clunked free and allowed her to push the door open. The sunshine flooded in with her. "Look at all the inventions!" She turned back to him with a look of surprise.

They were everywhere, catching the light, but Lexington said, "I don't even see them anymore. I'm always working on the next one."

She stood in that spot of sun and slowly looked around. There were the Rocket Shoes he made. That wasn't one of his better ideas. She was surrounded by them. A bicycle with spread feathered wings. A robot with eight arms resting on four typewriters. It wore a watch on each blue sleeve.

"There's the projector," he said. The cement booth was on a red wagon, easier to move around. "The star attraction…"

Forty years ago, they lowered that into Avalon Pond. It sat there like a treasure chest. Ida imagined its slow transformation into weeds and algae. "It was down there all this time," she marveled.

"You want to see the movie it was playing to get my attention?"

Her eyes jumped.

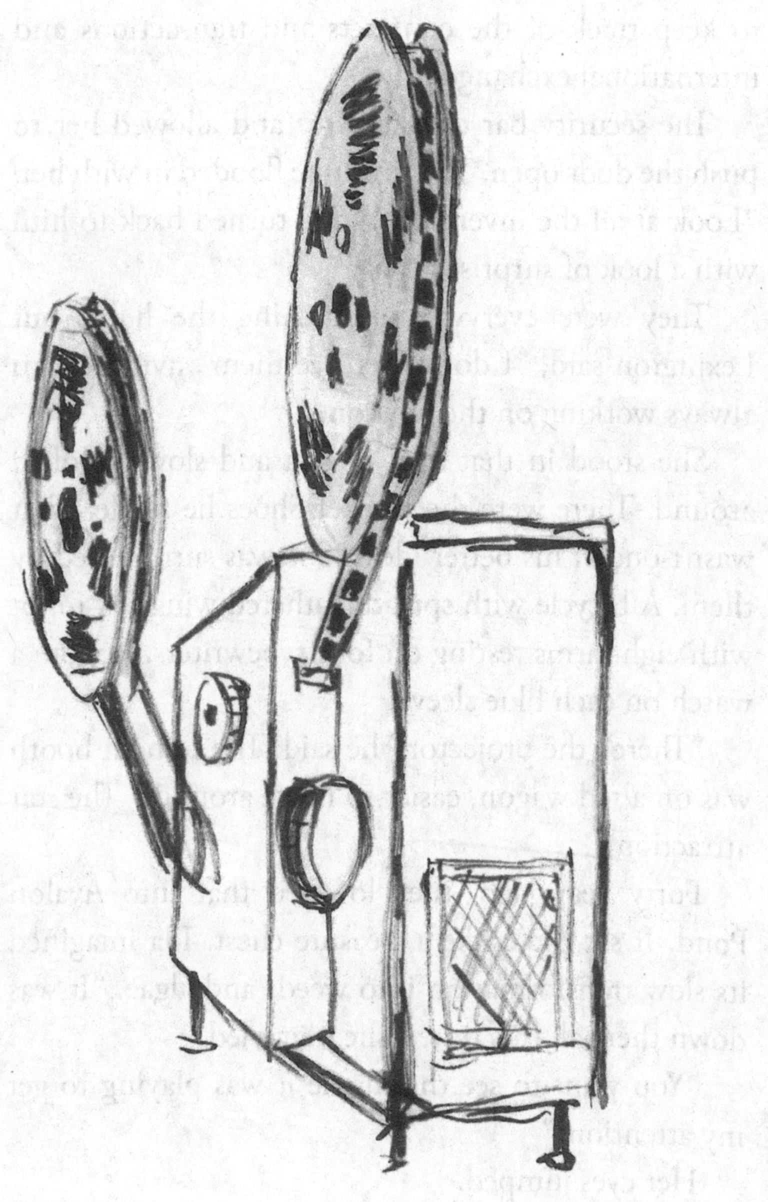

He laughed, "Remember all the movies we used to make?" Curly always wanted to be the villain, defeated by Ida every time. Lexington would sometimes make an appearance too. Once he wore a gorilla costume.

"Yes! Of course I want to see them!"

Lexington figured she would. It was the strangest magic to watch, hard to believe that much time had catapulted them all ahead…except for Curly. Lexington lit a candle near The Pond Projector. "Have a seat," he offered. There were a couple of mismatched chairs with a view of the screen rolled down on the opposite wall. He went back to the door and shut it. The only light was from the candle. Then Lexington turned the dial and sat down near her as the movie started. "Sorry, no popcorn."

An aquarium scene, a stream of bubbles, some goldfish, then a title in big letters, BATHYSPHERE ADVENTURE! A silver fishing weight descended— that was Ida's bathysphere. The next scene was inside, a set made of painted cardboard with a kitchen chair. Ida laughed and she laughed again when Curly appeared. An eleven-year-old Boris Karloff, the King of the Undersea World.

Five minutes and the movie was done. Ida had her eyes covered, pressing her palms. Lexington had found a dream she had when she was ten.

"We have a box full of them," Lexington said. He got up and went to his desk. The projector clicked and began to rewind the reel automatically. He looked in the box and took out, "JUNGLE ADVENTURE! This is the one where I was a gorilla." He picked up the next one and read, "HAUNTED HOUSE ADVENTURE!"

Ida laughed. "They're all titled some adventure, aren't they?"

"TEST PILOT ADVENTURE!"

She laughed.

"And each title has an exclamation point. That was Curly's contribution. He was into punctuation marks then."

Ida told Lexington she wanted to watch them all.

So they did.

The experience reminded her there was something she missed—she was glad for the life she had—but those childhood feelings and that freedom she had, the imagination they shared making those movies. That was Lexington Brown's idea to make movies. Adventures! She missed that fun. They had become other people with different lives, apart from each other. She couldn't miss Curly though. He was exactly the same. The strange case of Curly Bane was hard to explain.

It was dusk when the projector shut down.

On the way to the house, Lexington got Ida's suitcase from Jim McBrady.

"Do you still like spaghetti?" he asked her.

"ITALIAN ADVENTURE!" she replied. She drew her arm back like she had in that movie and threw an imaginary handful of spaghetti. In the movie it got the villain right in the face. "Poor Curly."

"He loved that scene. He's such a ham in those movies."

"What's going to happen to him now?"

Lexington opened the screen door. He said, "You could adopt him."

She laughed at his expression. "What would my husband say if I came home with an eleven-year-old? Why don't *you* adopt him?" And she laughed at Lexington's doubletake. "Why not? You've got this big house. He already knows his way around."

"Oh, I don't think so. I'm used to being alone." He set her suitcase by the stairway. "There's a guestroom upstairs. Come on through to the kitchen. I bet you're hungry."

"For spaghetti?"

He tapped his head, "You read my mind." All he had to do was boil some water for pasta, the sauce had been simmering all day. The table was set for two, the same red Formica table he wrote letters from when he was a boy.

She caught him up on the things she had done. He told her where he had been.

An unseen circle was filling in.

The sun was getting lower in the window, glowing in the leaves.

He looked at the clock. "Believe it or not, I have to go to work."

WILL CURLY BANE BE OKAY?

(Turn to page 94 for the solution to "Lexington Brown Sets the Stage")

LEXINGTON BROWN
GOES TO CITY HALL

Jim McBrady carried him back into town. The engine sound was turned down. He wanted to keep thinking about Ida and Curly. He left Ida back at home. She was on the couch, watching a repeat of *Murder Conductor*. He remembered her telling him when she grew up, she would be a great detective like Shelby Wills. She always liked detective shows. Jim Rockford and Angel Martin. He smiled. He sure enjoyed their long talk during dinner. When he told her he had to go to work, they got around to that subject.

"I'm a stenographer," Ida told him.

"Is that right?" he replied.

"Mmhmm. Graduate of the Stenography School of New Mexico." She told him more than he ever knew about stenography then she asked, "What about you? I suppose you've made ten thousand inventions."

"Yeah, well I'm lucky that way. That's what keeps me going, you might say. Everyone needs to do the real work they're meant to do. Now for my *day job*, I work at City Hall."

"Oh," she turned her head, "Mayor Brown?"

"No, nothing like that. I'm the nightshift custodian."

She didn't say anything. She was probably surprised that he wasn't in a lab or a wind-tunnel. What irony, he thought. Under his photo in the school yearbook was his name and one single word: GENIUS. The smartest kid in school and here he was pushing broom at the City Hall. Anyway, it wasn't bad. It gave him time to think. He had a lot of good ideas while he was there at night. Sometimes he would turn the floor buffer off so he could write something down. The real work stayed with him always.

The streetlights and store windows waltzed. It was like being in a phosphorous school of fish. City Hall was dark.

He went in the dull employee door at the back of the building. He followed the hall to his locker. He opened the metal door and took off his windbreaker and left it in there like a bat on a hanger. He got his blue vest and put it on over his plaid shirt.

Ready for work. His mop was parked where he left it in the corner.

With a fresh bucket of soapy water, Lexington pushed his way into the dark lobby.

It was a well-known rumor that City Hall had a ghost. If anyone joking around asked him about it and wanted to know if he saw it at night, he would roll his eyes and shake his head and say no. But he was well acquainted with the ghost, and he didn't mind its presence at all.

"You there, Ben?" he called into the empty room.

He reached through the darkness and found the lamp where he knew it would be. It spread light into the far reaches. He was alone.

The ghost must have been busy in some other world.

It didn't appear until Lexington was on the second floor, emptying an office garbage can.

"Well, well," Lexington smiled, "I was wondering when—"

......

Lexington was the only one who could hear Ben. Lexington listened to a voice in the quiet room answer him and start to ask a question. Lexington quickly explained, "No, I was downstairs in the—"

......

A moment later Lexington nodded, "That's right, the floor was a mess. They—"

......

"Oh, is that what happened?"

......

Anyone watching would've thought Lexington Brown was lost in the imaginary, talking to himself, or to some invisible telephone. "Who—"

......

"I should've known!" he laughed. "He—"

......

"No, that was last month. That's when she—"

......

"Every time!" he laughed. "I had to—"

......

"It was okay," he shook a hand over the mop bucket, "I just added a little—"

......

"Yes, it comes right out as long as you don't—"

......

Then he looked surprised, "You do? Is it that late? Let me see..." He lifted his sleeve to read his watch, "It's—"

......

"No, I won't keep you. I guess we better—"

......

Lexington smiled, "No problem at all, we both—"

......

When Lexington laughed, he admitted, "That's why I like talking with you, Ben. We understand each other so well." He waved, then whatever ghost he was talking to was gone.

Lexington placed the empty garbage can back by the desk and once he vacuumed his way out, he was done with the room. The City Hall had four floors that were in daily use. Carpeted halls with offices, a kitchen, four restrooms. It took him hours to clean thoroughly. Sometimes he would go up in the cupola to greet the dawn. It was one of the rarest views in town, looking over the red dragon scaled tiles of the tower to the bay with its islands just catching the sunrise.

And he kept one last unclean place for last before his shift was done.

The ghost wasn't the biggest secret at City Hall, or the scariest. Waiting downstairs in the basement, hidden inside file cabinets, things of far more horror were shut away. The evidence in letters, photos, newspapers, deeds and treaties, and ill-willed artifacts told the story of the town. It rattled like a dark nightmare, an unconscious howl that recalled in undisguised truth the violence from the start. From the moment the forests were ripped apart and the settlement drawn, a coil of tragedies unraveled. It came with the mines, the railroad, the labor bloodshed, the KKK, the politics and deals done behind this building's very doors. A malevolent plundering greed that also slaughtered the riches of animal life and poisoned their environment. The basement was filled with murder and terror. You could open any drawer. Read how the factory poured chlorine into the bay, their names and exploits were left buried in the silt. The room was trapped with all the lives that were caught in it from then until now. Those cabinets kept burning. Lexington could feel the power boiling like a fusion reactor.

He swept the cold concrete floor as quickly as he could and got out of the cellar and locked the door. If only Lexington Brown could come up with an invention to repair that haunted history. But it stayed in the dark and it beat like a coal black heart.

WHO ELSE KNEW THE CURSE OF THE VAULT?

*(Turn to page 96 for the solution to
"Lexington Brown Goes to City Hall")*

LEXINGTON BROWN
MAKES A SCENE

The town had twenty banks, one movie theater, a derelict factory, and it was home to a circus that hung on by the spokes of its wheels. The town had the usual number of gas stations, churches and schools, fast food, cafés and stores that lined Main and Holly. There were old, treed neighborhoods where you still saw deer, new concrete apartments that shot up overnight, and mansions along the water. But it only *looked* like an average American town…there are still some nooks and crannies where rare survivors of a dreamworld cling like flowers to a cliff. Lexington Brown was taking Ida to one of those places for breakfast.

It was still early morning with a pearl white sky that hadn't yet broken into blue.

Jim McBrady slowed.

"This is unreal…" said Lexington, "Look over there. I can't believe who it is!" So many things were coming together. It felt like Lexington was fit to a machine, an invention that could tie past and present together.

Ida twisted on the seat and put a hand to the window, "Is that—?"

"Yes!" Lexington said, "Poke Bleekers!"

Her hands couldn't help clenching into fists.

Lexington turned the steering wheel. "It most definitely is…"

Poke Bleekers was the terror of neighborhood kids long ago. He was always up to no good, forever bullying, scheming, and making life miserable. But as he came into view, Poke didn't look so tough anymore. His every step was a decision.

Jim McBrady fit into the painted lines next to Poke's car.

Ida said, "What are we going to do?" She held the buckled seatbelt. Lexington used to rely on her for muscle when Poke was around.

"I don't know…" Lexington opened the door, got out and let it close. What do you say to someone like Poke after all these years? Lexington never forgot the sneer, the push, the shove. "Excuse me," he called, "Poke?"

When Poke turned around, time fell away. It was

funny, how you could still tell it was him. Something in his eyes. The plaid suitcoat he wore was only a disguise.

"My name isn't Poke…It's Herbert. Herbert Bleekers. I sell insurance."

Lexington felt bad, stopping this old man before the State Farm office.

Herbert said, "Look, I have a job to do and I'm running a little late this morning." His eyes saw Ida behind the windshield. He knew it was them, but he didn't let on. He carried a folder full of paperwork, he was an important leader in the business community. Whatever he used to be, to him it was already forgotten

"Okay, sorry. I won't keep you…" Lexington backed off. He didn't know what he wanted to happen, not exactly. Back in the day, Poke would have pounded you if you called him Herbert. Now it was okay. Now he was just a hobbling phantom of what he was.

The windows of State Farm shined like a drive-in movie screen. Poke was going in, Lexington stood back watching, and behind him Jim McBrady was parked with other cars.

When Lexington got back into the cab and turned the key, Ida asked him, "What did he say?"

The Sonics returned. It was the third quarter. They

were down by seven.

"Not much." Lexington looked over his shoulder while he backed up. He sighed as he put the truck in drive.

"You look tired, Lex."

"I'm not." The truck carried them back onto the street. "I don't need much sleep. You know, Nikola Tesla only slept two hours a night. That's the way we inventors are wired."

The basketball game mumbled them along downtown. Ida admired the Avalon Theatre's stately tower, built in 1926 when the city could have been a skyline in Italy. And she thought about the pond they made and the movies that rayed in it. She never questioned Lexington Brown back then, every idea he had was gold.

Jim McBrady rumbled like a radio, "Sikma saves, lob to Gus…That was a good move by Gus, hold it out, use up the clock, you have to use the time up here." The street was slanted at the sea. A gull drifted overhead like a lazy kite to Kansas.

She didn't remember this part of town, her memories mostly took place at school, their neighborhood, the houses of friends. The truck parked in front of an antique store, so old it looked like an antique itself.

Everything in the window had the quiet grace of a photograph. The Golden Age Café was next door. A dog lay on the sidewalk like a mop halfway to water. It raised an eyebrow as they approached.

"I smell breakfast," Ida grinned. It floated out the open door and fainted dogs.

Just inside, Lexington paused by the notice board and pointed at the colorful poster. "Underwater Movies at the Aquarium," he read. "Presenting the first public debut of the adventurous films of local luminary, Lexington Brown. Shown as he intended with his Pond Projector."

"Local luminary," Ida said, and she squeezed his arm, "It's finally happening. Tonight!"

"I hope I'm ready," he said.

"Are you kidding me, Lex? You're ready. You have been ready. It's the world that took so long to be ready."

A waitress found them and escorted them through the crowded room to a table near the window. A girl played a banjo in the corner. A grasshopper sound, a sunny handful of notes she pulled from the strings. Lexington sat down wondering if a banjo could play underwater. Distracted by that thought, and Ida by the menu, they didn't notice who sat at the next table until he spoke.

"Lexington Brown, I presume?"

"Yes."

"Then I feel thankful that I am here to welcome you."

Lexington stared at the slumped man saluting them with a coffee cup. He tried vainly to conjure up an identity.

"And if I'm not mistaken, that's Ida Bell with you? How remarkable."

Ida, who was always there to help, said, "Arthur. Arthur Moon," and Arthur was pleased.

Arthur continued, "No doubt you two are married? I guess we all expected that."

Ida and Lexington both denied that quickly, they were just friends, that's all they ever were.

Arthur rolled his eyes and sipped at the last of his coffee.

Lexington couldn't believe it was Arthur Moon, another link to that childhood time, and more proof that his fate was converging. "Arthur Moon…How you doing? I thought you were—"

"No, not anymore."

"Oh, you—"

"For thirty years!" Arthur crowed. "Not bad for a C student, eh?" he glared at Lexington and then

Lexington remembered the boy Arthur Moon used to be and the way people were in school. "We can't all be the class genius," Arthur told him. "Life is hard for the rest of us. I'm afraid the rat race is our inescapable fate. I honestly still don't quite get why people think it has to be this way. I hope to heaven that we have a modicum of health and vitality left when we finally get to retire. I feel so awful for people who slave away the precious minutes and years, only to retire a ghost."

The waitress reappeared with coffee and poured two cups. "I like your dress," she told Ida. It was the first time Lexington saw Ida in a dress. Then the waitress took their breakfast orders and left.

"What do you know about that?" Arthur Moon gloomed, "A refill would have been nice. She ignored me. Perhaps I may be the product of having seen one too many ghosts."

Ida was looking out the window. Lexington turned his attention out there with her. It was always changing. The trees, the buildings, the cars, the people, they were like clouds that came and went. It was only in memories where the world stayed amber.

DID THEY ENJOY THEIR BREAKFAST?

(Turn to page 98 for the solution to "Lexington Brown Makes a Scene")

LEXINGTON BROWN
AT THE AQUARIUM

A mermaid played a harp in the aquarium lobby.

Lexington heard Ida tell him, "Oh, look at this place!" and she reminded him of someone at Disneyland. That's how it felt to him too. A mysterious dark room. Blue, green lights made waves across the ceiling. The harp soundtrack and the shadows of people moving with you, pulled towards something you could feel rushing ahead like a waterfall.

On either side of them were portholes in the wall. Weeds and fish encased in them, bubbles filling some. You could believe you were in a submarine and even the floor was taking you down.

"We're almost there," said Lexington. He spent the afternoon testing The Pond Projector. In between visits with luminaries and a *Herald* reporter intent on writing a story, he made sure his invention was working and he was excited to see what an audience would think, especially his two friends who had come all this way.

Curly held onto Ida and Lexington, walking between them in his pajamas. The white bathrobe he wore had black lettering on the back like a boxer: Fine's Self Storage. He was excited too. Everything to him was a dream.

The hallway opened into a room, a theater that was like being inside a round shell. Rows of seats went up at a slant, facing a window the size of the Avalon screen. A hundred fish swam round and round.

Once all the seats were filled, the lights dimmed, and everyone watched the water. A beautiful blue glow soft as a summer night, a school of sardines sparkling like stars. Then, while everyone watched, the projector began sending out a movie onto a coral ledge. Lexington remembered it, ANDES ADVENTURE! Curly's dog starred as a llama, Ida was Queen of the Incas. For a second, Lexington Brown's face glowed on the side of a shark. It was a spooky effect, as if the shark ate him and he was locked inside like Pinocchio. A sea turtle paddled into the movie moonbeam.

Lexington's Pond Projector was a window that showed the past, three kids playing, making up stories in another town in time. Seeing his dream come true, he was pleased every time Ida reacted, as she would laugh and look at him. Curly bounced between them. You didn't have to know the stars to be affected, the audience liked it too—and Lexington had to admit, the aquarium might have improved his invention—they didn't have to be in the water to watch the movie.

The Queen of the Incas waved goodbye from the painted mountains. The screen went dark for a moment as the projector with all its wheels and spooling arms safely encased in cement began the next movie, BATHYSPHERE ADVENTURE! Cardboard fish on sticks were met by real fish swimming past.

After three movies, the projector stopped. The houselights dawned and the reaction at the end took Lexington by surprise. Applause!

The aquarium president stood up from the front row and talked into a microphone, welcoming everyone. While she mentioned their anniversary and thanked each person and fish who made this place what it was, she pointed at the audience and picked out Lexington Brown, inventor of The Pond Projector. She called him down. She asked him to say something. So he stood and made his way through the clapping surf and the knees turned to let him get past to the aisle.

Lexington didn't know what he was going to say. He felt like a salmon tumbling down a rushing stream. He tried to think of something. The Pond Projector waited forty years for this.

When he met the president earlier, she didn't tell him this was going to happen. Now Gillian stood there smiling, holding out the microphone.

Lexington Brown took it and took a breath and said, "Thanks…"

He couldn't believe it. He was glad he wore his good suit. Though the sleeves were still wet with sea water. The room became quiet as all those people in rows waited for him to speak.

He wished he had written a speech. Or at least some notes on a scrap of paper.

"Thanks. Thanks for coming here tonight… Thanks to the aquarium for your interest in The Pond Projector. This means a lot to me. Like something I waited my whole life to see…I feel I was born to invent…I had my difficulties along the way, but now——"

That was as far as he got when a piercing shriek came from the woman beside the mayor in the front row. "My necklace is gone!"

The evening took a whole other turn from there. It

would soon become something from a Charlie Chan movie as the president attempted to calm everyone down, while also assuring that nobody should move from their seats. Everyone sat still, where they were, and she hissed to the interns to guard the doors. With all their excitement, it was the fishes' turn to look at them for entertainment. In half an hour the place would be crawling with police.

Before all that came to pass, an eleven-year-old man stood up from seat 20G. Curly raised his pajama arms and waved and yelled, "You'll figure it out, Lexington Brown! You're the smartest guy in town!"

HOW DID HE KNOW?

(Turn to page 100 for the solution to "Lexington Brown at the Aquarium")

Solution to "Lexington Brown, Dream Inventor"

Lexington Brown went to the library. While the tide of years had whirled around, changing everything, this place remained on the corner of Shirley Street. He breathed the cool air and smell inside. The windowlight and shadows reminded him of a calm ocean. Once he got between those shelves and started hunting for books, he could be lost for hours. One book led to another. The secrets of the world were there.

Today he was looking for a simple answer and he knew it would be where he went when he was ten. He followed the blue carpet trail to the Children's section and nearly bumped into his ghost on the wall, an old, framed photograph of a black and white boy reading. He was no different now, books told him what he needed to know.

In the middle of the room, a girl sat reading a book about a talking dog. She had gathered other books on the tabletop. It was reassuring to know this place was still teaching and drawing new disciples like a guru on a hill.

And sure enough, the right book was waiting for him. *The Golden Book of Levers, Pulleys, & Winches.* He clutched the soft bound covers. This would tell him how to get his invention out of Avalon Pond, across land, into the safety of his garage.

Solution to "Lexington Brown Takes on the Town"

Lexington opened the envelope, unfolded the letter, and read three words:

Try the publisher

Solution to "Lexington Brown Gathers the Gang"

An operator does still exist at the end of the "O" line. She was very helpful. It didn't take her long to find phone numbers for both Ida and Curly. Lexington wrote those on his paper. After he replaced the receiver, he stared at the numbers for a long time. So much lifetime had run between his friends and him. He last saw them in those childhood days. He never expected to be calling them. But now that the past had caught up with him in the form of The Pond Projector, he wanted his friends with him at the aquarium.

He called Ida first. She lived a thousand miles away, but he could picture her. When she answered, he gripped the 1940s telephone and for a moment he lost his voice like Pearl Harbor. The water was flecked with a coat of black dust and ghost white feathers. He couldn't believe it was her, not until he said her name and heard her say his name back.

When he called Curly, he got a recording. "I'm not here right now, leave a message." So Lexington did. Then he looked at the address he had written down. It was for White Pond, it wasn't far. Lexington couldn't wait to see the look on his old friend's face when he opened the door.

Solution to "Lexington Brown Reads the Signs"

One night, a week after the events of this book, Owen Feathers wandered in the warm, blue July night down Clover Avenue. He veered off the road, onto a deer path sunk in the weeds. It took him past a couple apple trees, right to Avalon Pond. The moon floated on the surface like a lily pad. He saw the chair near the reeds on the shore, a front row seat for the frog orchestra already in full swing. The moon in the pond called him closer. He tramped into the softened earth and then like that tightrope walker so many years ago, he walked fearlessly onto the narrow wooden pier. His weight barely pressed down as he stepped over the puddle in the middle and balanced to the end. That's where he kneeled on that creaking board, cupped his hands, and dipped them in the pond. He took a sip and as he stood back up, his mind became crystal clear. There are waters like this with healing properties where pilgrims come. Who knows how Owen knew what to do, or why it took a lifetime for him to discover Avalon Pond? All that mattered was the miracle they worked.

Solution to "Lexington Brown Travels in Time"

She expected the rattly wheeze of a sixty-year-old truck motor.

As soon as Lexington turned the key, the sound of the engine was, "Freddie Brown, Dennis Johnson, Jack Sikma, Paul Sylas, and John Johnson on the floor for Lenny Wilkins..." Jim McBrady turned swiftly onto the road and the broadcast got a little louder as he pressed the gas pedal.

Ida stared at the talking truck hood, "What?"

"I made a truck that runs on memory. The collective memory of the Seattle Sonics in their final championship game has energy. I could drive this truck to the moon on that." He turned down the applause with the radio dial and the truck hummed along.

Solution to "Lexington Brown & The Sleeping Kid"

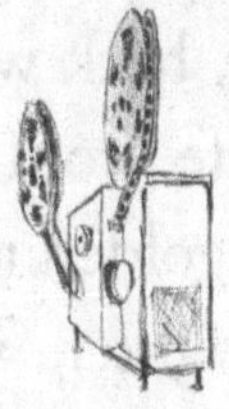

Seattle SuperSonics..............97

The Washington Bullets.......93

Solution to "Lexington Brown Sets the Stage"

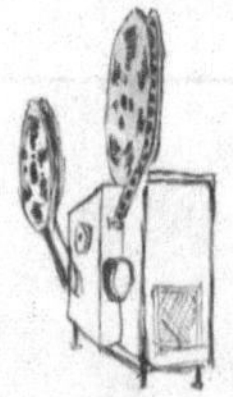

Good question! Some people say kids had it better growing up forty years ago, when there wasn't the same fear in the air, back when they roamed the neighborhoods free, safe from harm and everyone knew everyone. Ahhh, golden memories.

Were the colors brighter, was the food better, would certain smells haunt you in years to come? Were there more birds, more green places for hide-and-seek games, and at night were there more stars to be seen? Maybe that's just nostalgia that makes it seem that way. Lexington Brown knew it depends on who you talk to.

They were lucky. When they were ten, happiness was easy coming and going. The last sounds of kids playing in the neighborhood, the last birds singing, as all that was day was fading into distance, as twilight put everything to bed.

Curly wanted to keep sleeping in that dreamworld, but Lexington Brown knew it wouldn't do. Getting his friend to the aquarium was the first step. Think of everything he still had to experience. Good and bad, that was the way of life. Lexington Brown knew Curly would land on his feet, that's how his eleven-year-old friend always was. Who could be sure what would happen to him next? But he had just as good a chance now as anyone ever did.

Solution to "Lexington Brown Goes to City Hall"

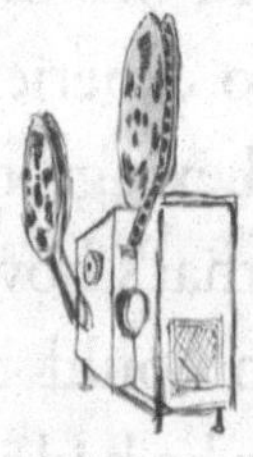

Everyone was haunted by that room, even if you didn't know history, even if you were in one of those mansions with a millionaire view of the sea. Out of the darkness, it kept transmitting, beaming like an unnamed living ghost. Growing up, Lexington Brown learned to beware of certain things, places, situations. Times would seem to get better, but it would never go away. Every so often he would feel it out on the streets of today. Sometimes only small, but sharp as the look in someone's eye.

It was dug deep in City Hall, rooted like one of those yellow cat's ear weeds so difficult to pull from his yard. And like a weed, it would stay. It made it hard to live in a world where that went on, but it made him want to find a way. You'd have to invent a whole new society. He wasn't the only inventor, it was a path, in life it was up to everyone to improve. The progress of being human is to do better, improve as a person, learn to do good.

Lexington wanted to believe something would come from it, that it wouldn't be a wound forever. The source of it was built into their everyday, but it was the bones, not the heart. There would always be the traumatic past but growing from that would be a flower.

Solution to "Lexington Brown Makes a Scene"

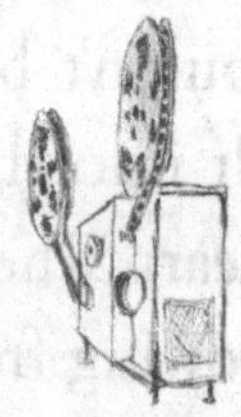

You better believe it! The Golden Age makes a terrific breakfast, and they even give free coffee refills (despite what Arthur Moon told them) and the bill wasn't bad either. Lexington retrieved his old leather wallet, the one he made in summer camp, soft now as floss, and paid.

On the street again, the sun had gained some ground, turning the sidewalk yellow. A phone booth loitered ahead. Ida reminded him they had to call Fine's Self Storage to arrange a taxi for Curly.

While Lexington stopped to dig into that wallet for change, Ida kneeled and searched through the cardboard FREE box in front of the antique store. There were things nobody would buy, some wooden milk bottle caps, a broken brass flower candleholder, a pair of empty glasses frames, a chipped painted plate, a plastic three-wheeled car. Then she laughed to herself as she found a present for Lexington. It was a beat-up paperback book, *The Love Letters of Phyllis Diller.*

Solution to "Lexington Brown at the Aquarium"

With the help of his Egyptian block and tackle, Lexington Brown raised The Pond Projector from the aquarium tank. It dripped like an anchor as he winched it down onto its red Radio Flyer wagon. He was behind the scenes, where you had to be an employee to go, surrounded by wheezing pipes and trestles. The movie premiere (if not for its sudden turn to crime) would have been a complete success. Lexington smiled anyway. He was ready to go home with his invention. First though, he and everyone else in the aquarium had to be searched by the police. All those people who had cheered for him were now slowed to a long sullen line like at an airport. Not the way to be memorable.

Unscrewing the last pin sealing the projection booth, Lexington carefully removed the hatch. The aquarium wanted copies of his movies—imagine that!—they had a special tank for them to be shown. A flock of minnows would wash in them.

The opened hatch let him see inside. His invention wrapped its film reels in metal arms protectively. There was also room in there for something else to shine. The pearl necklace, nacreous, iridescent, gleaming just like its beginning in an oyster shell.

How did the pearls end up in there? How much time had gone by earlier in the day, while Lexington left the projector unattended, gladhanding with the director and dignitaries? Enough time for a thief to hide the pearls in there. Nobody confessed, it didn't matter, they were all guests at the aquarium, they all could have done it. The important thing was the pearls were back. So it came to pass that Lexington Brown and his Pond Projector were celebrated a second time.

As for Ida and Curly, they'll be alright too. The three friends left each other that night. Ida flew back home and Curly went back to sleep. While down a quiet driveway next to a pond at 13 Clover Avenue, Lexington Brown had another invention idea.

LEXINGTON BROWN
& THE POND PROJECTOR
Written during June 2021

Books by Good Deed Rain

Saint Lemonade, Allen Frost, 2014. Two novels illustrated by the author in the manner of the old Big Little Books.

Playground, Allen Frost, 2014. Poems collected from seven years of chapbooks.

Roosevelt, Allen Frost, 2015. A Pacific Northwest novel set in July, 1942, when a boy and a girl search for a missing elephant. Illustrated throughout by Fred Sodt.

5 Novels, Allen Frost, 2015. Novels written over five years, featuring circus giants, clockwork animals, detectives and time travelers.

The Sylvan Moore Show, Allen Frost, 2015. A short story omnibus of 193 stories written over 30 years.

Town in a Cloud, Allen Frost, 2015. A three part book of poetry, written during the Bellingham rainy seasons of fall, winter, and spring.

A Flutter of Birds Passing Through Heaven: A Tribute to Robert Sund, 2016. Edited by Allen Frost and Paul Piper. The story of a legendary Ish River poet & artist.

At the Edge of America, Allen Frost, 2016. Two novels in one book blend time travel in a mythical poetic America.

Lake Erie Submarine, Allen Frost, 2016. A two week vacation in Ohio inspired these poems, illustrated by the author.

and Light, Paul Piper, 2016. Poetry written over three years. Illustrated with watercolors by Penny Piper.

The Book of Ticks, Allen Frost, 2017. A giant collection of 8 mysterious adventures featuring Phil Ticks. Illustrated throughout by Aaron Gunderson.

I Can Only Imagine, Allen Frost, 2017. Five adventures of love and heartbreak dreamed in an imaginary world. Cover & color illustrations by Annabelle Barrett.

The Orphanage of Abandoned Teenagers, Allen Frost, 2017. A fictional guide for teens and their parents. Illustrated by the author.

In the Valley of Mystic Light: An Oral History of the Skagit Valley Arts Scene, 2017. A comprehensive illustrated tribute. Edited by Claire Swedberg & Rita Hupy.

Different Planet, Allen Frost, 2017. Four science fiction adventures: reincarnation, robots, talking animals, outer space and clones. Cover & illustrations by Laura Vasyutynska.

Go with the Flow: A Tribute to Clyde Sanborn, 2018. Edited by Allen Frost. The life and art of a timeless river poet. In beautiful living color!

Homeless Sutra, Allen Frost, 2018. Four stories: Sylvan Moore, a flying monk, a water salesman, and a guardian rabbit.

The Lake Walker, Allen Frost 2018. A little novel set in black and white like one of those old European movies about death and life.

A Hundred Dreams Ago, Allen Frost, 2018. A winter book of poetry and prose. Illustrated by Aaron Gunderson.

Almost Animals, Allen Frost, 2018. A collection of linked stories, thinking about what makes us animals.

The Robotic Age, Allen Frost, 2018. A vaudeville magician and his faithful robot track down ghosts. Illustrated throughout by Aaron Gunderson.

Kennedy, Allen Frost, 2018. This sequel to *Roosevelt* is a coming-of-age fable set during two weeks in 1962 in a mythical Kennedyland. Illustrated throughout by Fred Sodt.

Fable, Allen Frost, 2018. There's something going on in this country and I can best relate it in fable: the parable of the rabbits, a bedtime story, and the diary of our trip to Ohio.

Elbows & Knees: Essays & Plays, Allen Frost, 2018. A thrilling collection of writing about some of my favorite subjects, from B-movies to Brautigan.

The Last Paper Stars, Allen Frost 2019. A trip back in time to the 20 year old mind of Frankenstein, and two other worlds of the future.

Walt Amherst is Awake, Allen Frost, 2019. The dreamlife of an office worker. Illustrated throughout by Aaron Gunderson.

When You Smile You Let in Light, Allen Frost, 2019. An atomic love story written by a 23 year old.

Pinocchio in America, Allen Frost, 2019. After 82 years buried underground, Pinocchio returns to life behind a car repair shop in America.

Taking Her Sides on Immortality, Robert Huff, 2019. The long awaited poetry collection from a local, nationally renowned master of words.

Florida, Allen Frost, 2019. Three days in Florida turned into a book of sunshine inspired stories.

Blue Anthem Wailing, Allen Frost, 2019. My first novel written in college is an apocalyptic, Old Testament race through American shadows while Amelia Earhart flies overhead.

The Welfare Office, Allen Frost, 2019. The animals go in and out of the office, leaving these stories as footprints.

Island Air, Allen Frost, 2019. A detective novel featuring haiku, a lost library book and streetsongs.

Imaginary Someone, Allen Frost, 2020. A fictional memoir featuring 45 years of inspirations and obstacles in the life of a writer.

Violet of the Silent Movies, Allen Frost, 2020. A collection of starry-eyed short story poems, illustrated by the author.

The Tin Can Telephone, Allen Frost, 2020. A childhood memory novel set in 1975 Seattle, illustrated by author like a coloring book.

Heaven Crayon, Allen Frost, 2020. How the author's first book *Ohio Trio* would look if printed as a Big Little Book. Illustrated by the author.

Old Salt, Allen Frost, 2020. Authors of a fake novel get chased by tigers. Illustrations by the author.

A Field of Cabbages, Allen Frost, 2020. The sequel to The Robotic Age finds our heroes in a race against time to save Sunny Jim's ghost. Illustrated by Aaron Gunderson.

River Road, Allen Frost, 2020. A paperboy delivers the news to a ghost town. Illustrated by the author.

The Puttering Marvel, Allen Frost, 2021. Eleven short stories with illustrations by the author.

Something Bright, Allen Frost, 2021. 106 short story poems walking with you from winter into spring. Illustrated by the author.

The Trillium Witch, Allen Frost, 2021. A detective novel about witches in the Pacific Northwest rain. Illustrated by the author.

Cosmonaut, Allen Frost, 2021. Yuri Gagarin stars in this novel that follows his rocket landing in an American town. Midnight jazz, folk music, mystery and sorcery. Illustrated by the author.

Thriftstore Madonna, Allen Frost, 2021. 124 summer story poems. Illustrated by the author.

Half a Giraffe, Allen Frost, 2021. A magical novel about a counterfeiter and his unusual, beloved pet. Illustrated by the author.

Lexington Brown & The Pond Projector, Allen Frost, 2022. An underwater invention takes three friends through time. Illustrated by Aaron Gunderson.